From the movie
Disney
FROZEN

OLAF'S NIGHT BEFORE CHRISTMAS

PaRragon

Bath • New York • Cologne • Melbourne • Delhi
Hong Kong • Shenzhen • Singapore • Amsterdam

’Twas the night before Christmas and all through the house,
not a creature was stirring, not even a mouse.

Stockings were hung by the chimney - but why?
Had they got wet? Were they left there to dry?

Elsa was sleeping all snug in her bed,
while glittering northern lights
danced overhead.

Anna snored softly
while I counted sheep ...

... settling myself in for
a COSY night's sleep.

When out on the fjord there arose such a Clatter,

I sprang from my bed to see what was the matter!

Away to the window I tumbled and rolled.
I pulled it wide open and – brrrr – was it cold!
A full moon was out and it lit up the night,
while snow flurries made the world sparkly and white!

Then, grabbing an icicle, what did I spy?
Eight little Svens flying high in the sky!
The Svens pulled a sleigh. There was someone inside.
Could Sven and Kristoff be out for a ride?

Straight towards the castle the flying
sledge came, while the man - was it Kristoff? -
called out some strange names:

"Now, Dasher! Now, Dancer! Now, Prancer and Vixen!
On, Comet! On, Cupid! On, Donner and Blitzen!
To the top of the turret and over the wall!
Now, dash away! Dash away! Dash away all!"

He sounded SO funny. Who was this big guy?

What was a turret, and how could Svens fly?

And then with a ringing
I heard on the roof
the thumping and bumping
of each little hoof.

Then from behind me,
there came a strange sound.
The whole chimney shook
as two feet hit the ground!

For SANTA

His boots were all black
and his trousers all red.
But where was the rest of him?
Where was his head?!

Then out of the fireplace
the man's face appeared.
He had kind, crinkly eyes
and a fluffy white beard.

Kristoff he wasn't;
this man smelled too nice.
Like snowballs and cookies
and Christmassy spice.

He placed a large bag filled with gifts on the floor.

Was there a sale on at Old Oaken's store?

He brushed off his clothes, then began to unpack,
pausing for KRUMKAKE left out as a snack.

This stranger had presents
for Anna and Sven,
for Kristoff, for Elsa
- for all of my friends!

I reached for his coat
and gave two little tugs.
I said, "My name's Olaf
and I like warm hugs!"

He turned with a start, then let out such a giggle,
I had to laugh, too, when I saw how he jiggled!

He gave me a hug:
such a wonderful gift.
Then he rose up the chimney,
all lively and swift.

And I heard him call out
as he flew out of sight ...